♡ The Wildwood Bakery ♡

Read more OWL DIARIES books!

OWL DIARIES

♥ The Wildwood Bakery ♥

Rebecca
Elliott

BRANCHES

SCHOLASTIC INC.

For Maisy and Katie, who have the
coolest wingchairs around. — R.E.

Special thanks to Eva Montgomery.

Library of Congress Cataloging-in-Publication Data
Names: Elliott, Rebecca, author. | Elliott, Rebecca. Owl diaries ; 7.
Title: The Wildwood Bakery / Rebecca Elliott.
Description: First edition. | New York : Branches/Scholastic Inc., 2017. |
Series: Owl diaries ; 7 | Summary: Macy's little sister has wings that are
too small, so Eva's class decides to raise money to buy her a flying
chair, and half the class opens a bakery, and the other half opens a candy
store—but soon competition between the two stores becomes more important
than their goal, and Eva needs to convince the other owls that they will
collect more money if everyone works as a team.
Identifiers: LCCN 2017015799 | ISBN 9781338163001 (pbk.) | ISBN 9781338163018
(hardcover)
Subjects: LCSH: Owls—Juvenile fiction. | Elementary schools—Juvenile
fiction. | Money-making projects for children—Juvenile fiction. |
Bakeries—Juvenile fiction. | Cooperativeness—Juvenile fiction. |
Diaries—Juvenile fiction. | CYAC: Owls—Fiction. | Schools—Fiction. |
Fund raising—Fiction. | Bakers and bakeries—Fiction. |
Cooperativeness—Fiction. | Diaries—Fiction.
Classification: LCC PZ7.E45812 Wi 2017 | DDC [Fic]—dc23 LC record available at https://
lccn.loc.gov/2017015799

10 9 8 7 6 5 4 3 2   17 18 19 20 21

Printed in the U.S.A.   40
First edition, November 2017

Book design by Marissa Asuncion
Edited by Katie Carella

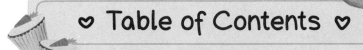

♡ Table of Contents ♡

♥ Well, Hello There! ♥

Sunday

Hello Diary,
    Did you miss me? It's me — Eva Wingdale! I wonder what exciting adventure we'll have this week!

I love:

Granny Owlberta's
cookies

The word
bubble

Saving up my
moon dollars

Funny jokes

Squirrels

Baby Mo's
laugh

Helping others

Winning at
WINGBALL

I DO NOT love:

 Stinky cheese

Rain clouds

 Baby Mo's cry

 Cleaning my room

Washing my wings
before I eat

The word gr<u>a</u>y

Mom's slug stew

Losing at
WINGBALL

My family is **FLAPERIFFIC**!

Here is a picture of us on Warm Hearts Day:

Dad

Mom

Me

Baby Mo

Humphrey

We all love Baxter – my cute pet bat.

I'm so lucky to be an owl. Owls do the best stuff. . .

We are awake when the sun has gone to bed.

We fly like superheroes.

We make super loud <u>hoot</u> sounds.

HOOT!

And we hatch out of eggs when we're chicks!

This is my tree house.

I live next door to my best friend EVER, Lucy Beakman. We sit together in Mrs. Featherbottom's class.

Here is our class photo:

George
Zac
Mrs. Featherbottom
Lilly
Jacob
Kiera
Sue
Hailey
Macy
Me
Zara
Lucy
Carlos

I can't wait to see all my friends at school tomorrow! Better get some sleep. Good day, Diary!

♡The Wingchair Plan♡

Monday

Today, Mrs. Featherbottom asked us each to share something we did over the weekend.

I played cards with Granny Owlberta and Grandpa Owlfred.

I made a model of the Owlpire State Building!

I sewed a new dress — with my mom's help.

I took photos of the sunset.

I visited my big brother in Owlahoma City.

I read the new Owl Ninja book.

I practiced playing my owlaphone.

I went to Brown Bear Mall with my little sister, Mia. We bought her a school bag.

Just then, I had a **FLAP-TASTIC** idea!

We could all raise the money for Mia's wingchair!

Eva, that's a splendid idea!

Class, your homework tonight is to think of the best fund-raising idea!

After school, Lucy came over, and we baked cookies.

Then I had ANOTHER **FLAP-TASTIC** IDEA – and so did Lucy! Both at the same time!

I'm SO excited! I can't wait to tell everyone our idea tomorrow!

♥ Yummy Scrummy ♥

Tuesday

School was such a **HOOT** today, Diary! Mrs. Featherbottom asked us to share our fund-raising ideas.

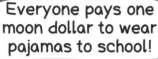
Everyone pays one moon dollar to wear pajamas to school!

We could sell our paintings!

A stay-awake-a-thon!

A magic show!

This half of the class will join Sue's group, and that half will join Eva and Lucy's group. You'll spend the week getting your shops ready!

Both shops will be at the Old Oak Tree, and they'll be open Saturday and Sunday. Together, we'll raise the money Mia needs in no time!

We all cheered.

At lunch, we sat in our groups.

It took us AGES to come up with a name . . .

Sugar Dreams?

Flaporrific Fancies?

The Nutty House?

The Crazy Cake Cottage?

I've got it! The Wildwood Bakery.

We all LOVED Macy's idea.

25

Next, we made a list of everything we need to do before Saturday:

1. Design our shop sign
2. Make flyers to advertise the shop
3. Bake cookies to sell
4. Decorate shop bags
5. Make garlands for inside the shop

After school, we went to my tree house to bake. But the cookie batter didn't taste good. So we used it for a food fight instead!

We'll have to bake FOR REAL tomorrow...

♡ Granny to the Rescue! ♡

Wednesday

Diary, sometimes Sue can be nice and sometimes Sue can be, well, Sue. Today, Sue was being Sue.

We're going to sell SO MANY of our super-tasty candies. No one will have any money left to spend at your bakery.

Don't be so sure, Sue. Our cookies are going to be BIG sellers, too.

During class, both teams worked on shop signs. Zac came up with ours.

We copied it to make our Wildwood Bakers membership cards.

At recess, I called our first secret Wildwood Bakers meeting. Everyone showed their cards and said the password. It was such a **HOOT**!

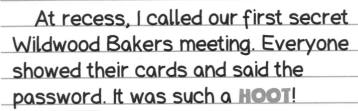

We have a great bakery name and sign!

Now we just need great cookies to sell.

The cookie batter we made last night was . . . well . . .

It was gross!

We need something REALLY special to sell in our shop.

What can we bake?

30

Everyone looked at me like I was crazy.

I've just had the BEST idea! My granny is an expert baker. I'm sure she'll help us! Everyone who can come — bring flour and sugar to my granny's house tonight!

Later, we told Granny Owlberta and Grandpa Owlfred about our shop.

We baked YUMMY cookies.

Then Hailey thought she saw someone at the window.

Look!

We flew outside.

No one was there. But Macy found something.

Hey, look at this!

It's a membership card!

Someone from Candy Crunch Corner was here!

They must be spying on us!

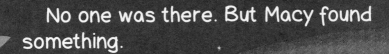

We flew back inside.

I bet they're trying to steal our ideas!

We HAVE to raise more money than them!

Yes, we have to win!

Calm down, owlets. Try not to worry about what other owls are doing. Just do your best. That's all any of us can do.

Granny is a very wise old owl. In order to do our BEST though, we'll need more than a cookie recipe.

Granny, do you have a really great cupcake recipe?

I have one that is _very_ special.

She took a dusty recipe book down from a shelf.

This is an old Wingdale Family recipe. These Dreamy Creamy Carrot Cupcakes are _so_ good, it is impossible to eat just one.

Legend has it that your Great-Great-Grandpa Wingston once ate so many Dreamy Creamies that he couldn't fly for a month!

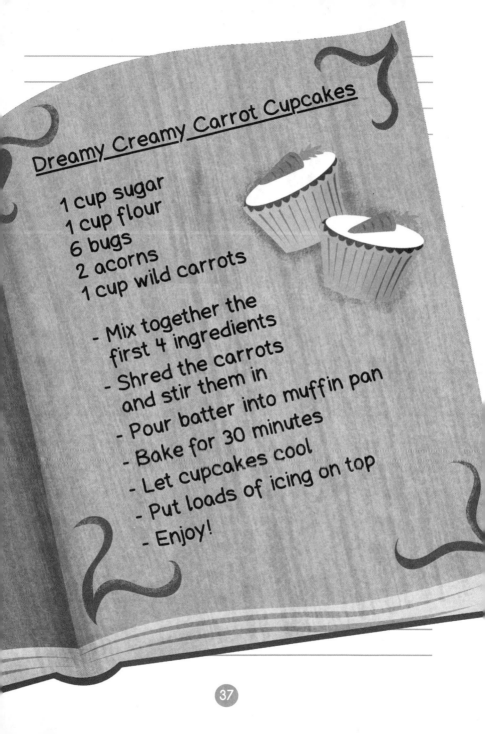

Dreamy Creamy Carrot Cupcakes

1 cup sugar
1 cup flour
6 bugs
2 acorns
1 cup wild carrots

- Mix together the first 4 ingredients
- Shred the carrots and stir them in
- Pour batter into muffin pan
- Bake for 30 minutes
- Let cupcakes cool
- Put loads of icing on top
- Enjoy!

Then Granny whispered:

Hard. But not impossible.
It's too late tonight but . . .
when you can, follow the
rabbits. Just don't let them
see you because they won't
like you taking their carrots!
Dress in dark clothes
to stay hidden.

Everyone said good-bye to Granny
and Grandpa. Then we all flew home.

Diary, tomorrow we are going to
find those wild carrots and bake those
Dreamy Creamies!
It's the ONLY
way we'll win.

♥ Ninja Carrot Hunters ♥

Thursday

When we got to school, everyone was whispering about secret plans for the shops. Sue was listening in on us. Again. It made me a bit mad.

I know you were spying on us last night, Sue!

Don't be silly, Eva. Why would I do that? We have the very best ideas for our shop.

Well, we have a top-secret recipe now. So our shop is definitely going to win!

We'll just see about that!

Mrs. Featherbottom called Sue and me over to her desk.

Now, girls, let's remember the most important thing is that your shops are raising money for Macy's little sister, Mia, and her special chair. I don't want to hear any more talk about winning.

I knew Mrs. Featherbottom was right. But I also still REALLY wanted our shop to raise more money than Sue's.

I called another secret Wildwood Bakers meeting.

When the Wildwood Bakers met up, we all looked so cool!

We flew around the forest looking for a rabbit.

We followed the rabbit to a patch of wild carrots. We hid in a tree and kept really quiet.

What now? Do we just take their carrots?

Those are <u>wild</u> carrots — they don't belong to the rabbits.

But still . . . We should ask before taking them.

I'll go talk to the rabbits. Wait here.

My friends flew down, and we picked wild carrots together.

Back at my tree house, we baked the Dreamy Creamies.

We baked SO MANY that we used up all our sugar!

Dad was our first taste tester.

These cupcakes are flaperrific! Can I have another?

I think you've had enough.

Granny did say that one is never enough!

Oh, go on then. But only if I can have one, too!

Diary, my bedroom is FILLED with cookies and cupcakes. YUM!

♥ Emergency Meeting ♥

Friday

Hi Diary,
    I cannot believe it's already Friday!
Our shop opens tomorrow!!

At recess today, we had fun playing **WINGBALL**. But the nets, uniforms, and balls are so old they're falling apart.

Our school <u>really</u> needs new wingball stuff!

I know, and it's too bad because my little sister loves wingball. It's one of the reasons she is looking forward to starting school.

Just then, Sue's team flew over.

Is Wildwood Bakery ready for its grand opening, Eva?

Yes, thank you. What about Candy Crunch Corner?

Of course.

We've got the best logo.

We've got the best candies.

Our cookies are owlmazing!

Our candy canes are the best in the world.

Then Sue said:

We passed out flyers, but we haven't seen any of yours. You'll be lucky if you get one customer!

ARGHHHHH!!!

Oh no! We should've made our flyers days ago!!

I called an emergency meeting at lunchtime. We looked at our to-do list:

1. Design our shop sign
2. Make flyers to advertise the shop
3. Bake cookies to sell and cupcakes
4. Decorate shop bags
5. Make garlands for inside the shop

There's still so much to do!

How did we forget about the flyers? Now no one knows about our shop!

Don't worry. We'll get it all done. Let's meet after school. Okay?

My little sister, Mia, wants to help. Can she come?

Of course! We need all the helping wings we can get!

After school, we worked hard.

Lucy and I made the garlands.

Zac and Hailey made the flyers.

George, Macy, and Mia decorated the bags. (We were lucky Mia helped out!)

We got everything ready in no time.

Next, we flew around the forest. We left a flyer on every doorstep so EVERYONE would know about our shop.

I can't wait for tomorrow!

7

♥ Cupcakes vs. Candy ♥

Saturday

We flew to the Old Oak Tree super early. We decorated our shop and put out the cupcakes and cookies.

Customers were lined up outside. Our families and friends and neighbors were all there!

Finally, it was
time to open the shop.

Oh my, Diary! Running
a bakery is hard work . . .

We had to get the cupcakes and
cookies for everyone.

We had to bag
them up.

And we had
to charge the
right amount of
moon dollars.

I took a quick peek at Candy Crunch Corner. Sue's shop seemed to have just as many owls in it as ours. So I wasn't sure who was winning.

At the end of the night, we were closing up when . . .

DISASTER!!!

We huddled together.

Let's think. What can we do?

We could ask Sue's team if we could borrow some sugar. They have lots of it for their candy recipes.

We can't ask <u>them</u> for help!

But if we don't, we'll have to close our shop.

And then Sue's team will win!

Everyone was quiet. We were all thinking hard about this decision.

If borrowing sugar helps us raise more money and win, then we should do it!

We flew to Candy Crunch Corner. Sue's team was all in a **FLAP** – just like we were!

Just then, we heard Mia's voice behind us.

I don't think I want a wingchair anymore. I thought these shops were supposed to be a fun way to help me. But the two teams aren't even friends anymore, and all you guys seem to want to do is win.

Everyone felt bad. We had forgotten why we were doing this in the first place. We had also forgotten we were all friends. And friends help one another.

Mrs. Featherbottom came to see how our shops had done in their first night. She counted up the moon dollars.

Both shops did very well — SO well that we have <u>already</u> raised enough money for Mia's wingchair!

Wow!

That's owlmazing! Thank you so much, everyone!

Mia and her Dad flew off.

We're so thankful to you all. Mia, let's go buy your new wingchair!

We told Mrs. Featherbottom our plan to put both shops together. She loved it!

We all flew to Sue's house to bake. We had a **FLAPERRIFIC** time!

When I got home, Humphrey burst into my room.

How's the bakery, Eva? Save any treats for me?

I did actually. Here you go.

Oh no!

What is it?

I forgot to take cupcakes to the rabbits who gave us the carrots!

So, Diary, I've set my alarm for super early tomorrow. I'm so tired . . .

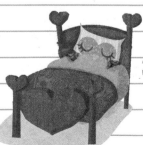

♥ The Wingball Champion! ♥

I flew to the rabbits' carrot patch when it was still light.

Thank you so much for helping us. Here are cupcakes just for you.

Wow, these are <u>hopperrific!</u>

Really yummy!

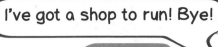

The new Wildcandy Cake Shop was a big success tonight! We had so much fun working together! After we closed up our shop, we ate the leftover treats.

Then Mia flew – yes, FLEW – in on her new wingchair!

Mia swooped up to catch it. She moved faster than any owl I've ever seen!

Wow, Mia!

It looks like the Treetop Owlementary wingball team has a new star player!

We all cheered! This was such a great week, Diary. See you next time!

Rebecca Elliott was a lot like Eva when she was younger: She loved making things and hanging out with her best friends. Now that Rebecca is older, not much has changed — except that her best friends are her husband, Matthew, and their children. She still loves making things, like stories, cakes, music, and paintings. But as much as she and Eva have in common, Rebecca cannot fly or turn her head all the way around. No matter how hard she tries.

Rebecca is the author of JUST BECAUSE and MR. SUPER POOPY PANTS. OWL DIARIES is her first early chapter book series.

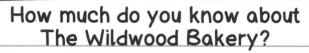

OWL DIARIES

How much do you know about The Wildwood Bakery?

What is a <u>wingchair</u>? How is it similar to a <u>wheelchair</u>? Why does Mia need one?

Look at page 43. Why are the Wildwood Bakers dressed like ninjas?

What is the disaster that happens at the end of the Wildwood Bakery's first night?

Mia uses a special wingchair to fly. Do you know anyone who uses something special to help them?

How is the Wildcandy Cake Shop formed? Use details to describe the thoughts, feelings, and actions of Eva and her classmates.